DISCARD

Stalking

Stalking

A Hot Issue

David Goodnough

Enslow Publishers, Inc.

40 Industrial Road	PO Box 38
Box 398	Aldershot
Berkeley Heights, NJ 07922	Hants GU12 6BP
USA	UK

http://www.enslow.com

Library of Congress Cataloging-in-Publication Data

Goodnough, David.
    Stalking / David Goodnough.
        p. cm. — (Hot Issues)
    Includes bibliographical references and index.
    Summary: Examines the invasive act of stalking, discussing the
motives and capabilities of the perpetrators, including stories of
people who have been stalked, and stressing the need for stronger
legal action against this crime.
    ISBN 0-7660-1364-2
    1. Stalking—United States Juvenile literature. [1. Stalking.]
I. Title. II. Series.
HV6594.2.G66   2000
364.15—dc21   99-37355
                                     CIP

Printed in the United States of America

10 9 8 7 6 5 4 3 2 1

To Our Readers:
All Internet addresses in this book were active and appropriate when we
went to press. Any comments or suggestions can be sent by e-mail to
Comments@enslow.com or to the address on the back cover.

Illustration Credits: AP/Wide World Photos, pp. 11, 15, 18, 25, 31,
41, 43, 52, 54; © Corel Corporation, p. 3; Skjold Photographs,
pp. 35, 37.

Cover Illustration: The Stock Market / © 1997 Jon Feingersh

Contents

1 The Crime of the Nineties— and Beyond 7

2 Who Are the Stalkers? 14

3 Anatomy of a Stalker 22

4 The Victims of Stalkers 28

5 Stalked and Stalking Teenagers 33

6 Celebrity Stalkers 39

7 Stalking and the Law 45

8 What to Do If You Are Stalked 51

Where to Find Help 58

Chapter Notes 59

Further Reading 63

Index 64

Chapter 1

The Crime of the Nineties— and Beyond

Barbara Wickens feels that her physical and mental health has been affected by something that happened when she was fifteen years old. She was stalked by a thin, middle-aged, balding man whom she and her high school friends knew only as "Creepy." He approached her in front of her town's public library and called her by name. He told her he wanted to be her friend. She had the good sense to run away, but that did not discourage her new "friend." Barbara was popular and attractive. She wanted to be a model and had appeared in a local fashion show. Her picture had been printed in the newspaper. She was easy to track down.

Creepy began following Barbara everywhere in his beat-up red car. She was constantly aware of his presence. She could not feel relaxed or safe anywhere. She was even afraid to go home when she knew she would be alone there. Creepy eventually showed up on her front porch. Barbara says she nearly fainted before slamming the door in his face and calling for her father. She hid in the back of her house while her father told the man that his daughter was definitely not interested in him and that he should leave her alone. Her father later notified the police, who said that Creepy was well known to them from previous complaints. They could not do anything except keep an eye on him, because he had not done Barbara any physical harm. There was no way of measuring the psychological harm he had done to her.

Barbara graduated from high school and went on to college. She gradually lost her fear and uneasiness. Eventually, she could even joke about her experience with Creepy. But then she began reading about other victims of stalkers. These girls and women had been attacked, raped, and even murdered by men who acted very much as Creepy had. Barbara began to wonder how she had escaped such a fate, or what would have happened had she remained in her hometown. She once again put herself in a constant state of alert. She now admits that she suffers from bouts of depression. She is not sure that Creepy is the cause of all this. "But," she says, "one thing I can say: he stole something very precious from me—my faith in the male half of humanity—and I have spent a lifetime trying to find it again."[1]

A veteran police officer and authority on the crime of stalking, Captain Robert L. Snow, puts Barbara's experience another way: "Stalking is one of the most psychologically crippling things that can happen to a person. Being stalked takes away a person's freedom, a person's security, and often a person's will to live."[2]

Stalking Defined

Stalking is the deliberate following or pursuit of one person by another over a period of time. It is threatening and possibly dangerous. It may cause

Stalking: A Legal Definition

Any person who(se):

(a) purposely engages in a course of conduct directed at a specific person that would cause a reasonable person to fear bodily injury to himself or herself or a member of his or her immediate family or to fear death of himself or herself or a member of his or her immediate family: and

(b) has knowledge or should have knowledge that the specific person will be placed in reasonable fear of bodily injury to himself or herself . . . (etc);

(c) acts induce fear in the specific person or bodily injury to himself or herself or a member of his or her immediate family or induce fear in the specific person of the death of himself or herself or a member of his or her immediate family;

is guilty of *stalking*.

Source: U.S. Department of Justice, *Project to Develop a Model Anti-Stalking Code for States* (Washington, D.C.: U.S. Government Printing Office, October 1993), pp. 43–44.

the pursued person to feel fearful for his or her safety. The stalker knows what he or she is doing, does it repeatedly, and his or her actions are frightening to the person being stalked.[3] Stalking is not new, but it has only recently been considered a crime. The first stalking law was passed in California in 1990. If stalking is brought to the attention of the general public, it is usually through incidents involving celebrities. Newspapers, magazines, and television news programs are quick to report any incidents of stalking involving actors, singers, politicians, or other celebrities. The criminal justice system has taken note of this increased awareness of the problem of stalking, and most states now have laws dealing with it.

Stalking in the News

Television talk show host David Letterman was stalked for years by a woman who claimed to be his wife. She even broke into Letterman's home and lived there while he was away. Tennis star Monica Seles was stabbed by a man who was stalking her rival Steffi Graf. The stalker had hoped to do away with Graf's competition by disabling Seles. The singer and actress Madonna was stalked by a man who showed up at her Hollywood mansion and threatened to "slit her throat from ear to ear" before a security guard shot and wounded him.[4] Television star Rebecca Schaeffer was murdered by an armed man who had rung her doorbell and delivered a fan letter earlier that day. "I worshiped her," he said after his capture.[5] In March 1998, a thirty-one-year-old man was convicted of stalking and plotting to rape and torture the filmmaker Steven Spielberg. He was arrested after he made two attempts to enter the Spielberg home.

One of the most notorious stalkers, the one who first brought widespread attention to this crime, was Mark David Chapman. He was the man who stalked and finally shot John Lennon on December 7, 1980, as Lennon was walking with his wife outside his apartment building in New York. There was also John Hinckley, Jr., who shot and wounded President Ronald Reagan in 1981. Hinckley had been stalking film star Jodie Foster, and tried to assassinate the president in order to impress her.

*R*obert Dewey Hoskins, left, had threatened to slit singer Madonna's throat. Here, Hoskins sits next to his lawyer as he is sentenced to ten years in prison for stalking and terrorizing the pop star.

Celebrities are not the only victims of stalkers. In fact, they represent only a small percentage of the number of men and women who are stalked daily. The National Institute of Justice (NIJ) estimates that 8 percent of women and 2 percent of men have been stalked at some point in their lives.[6] These percentages represent more than 10 million people in the United States. A survey conducted by the NIJ found that most victims are acquainted with their stalker. Women are more likely to be stalked by a former spouse, a former lover, or a former dating partner. Only 21 percent of women who are stalked do not know their tormentors, whereas most men are stalked by a complete stranger or a slight acquaintance. Women were usually stalked by a person acting alone. Men were usually the victim of a stalker and an accomplice.[7]

Most stalking goes unreported or little noticed, since it usually involves former dating partners or spouses. Unless real harm is done or the person being stalked is threatened, the case probably goes unreported. Judging from the number of reported cases, however, police have estimated that there are more than one hundred fifty thousand stalkers in the United States alone.[8] Many other law enforcement officials make much higher estimates.

Law enforcement agencies are poorly equipped to deal with the threat that these people impose. However, attempts are being made to identify stalkers and either stop them before or punish them after an actual crime has been committed. The laws that treat stalking differ from state to state. Activities that are punishable with a prison sentence in one state may be treated only as a misdemeanor in another.

Antistalking Laws

Following the public outcry over well-publicized stalking cases, all fifty states passed laws against stalking. Some were very strict, coming down hard on offenders. Others were more lenient, letting stalking activity go unpunished as long as no physical harm has been done to the victim. Obviously, some broad guidelines were needed.

Starting in 1994, Congress passed a series of laws designed to make stalking a federal crime. Since most of the victims of stalkers are women, the laws are known as the Violence Against Women Act (VAWA). The new laws made stalking a crime punishable by up to five years in prison. However, most victims, law enforcement agencies, legal authorities, researchers, and commentators agree that the laws do not go far enough in protecting against stalking situations.[9]

Chapter 2

Who Are the Stalkers?

Eighty-seven percent of stalkers are men.[1] Even stalkers of men are usually male. John Lennon's murderer and President Reagan's unsuccessful assassin were also men. Both were driven by a desire for attention and public recognition. This is one of the forces that drives a stalker.

Another characteristic of the stalker is the close identification of the stalker with the victim. Since President Reagan and John Lennon were famous, it shows that the stalker had an intense interest in celebrity and in the media. This is a common factor in most cases of stalking of celebrities. However, it does not explain the stalking of ordinary men and women who have little claim to fame or are hardly newsworthy.

Many stalkers of ordinary people are the victims' coworkers or social acquaintances. They may have socialized with them casually outside their workplace or even dated them. In some cases, the stalkers have even lived with or been married to their victims. These stalkers are usually characterized as being obsessive in their relationships. They are so fascinated and involved with the object of their obsession that they can think of little else. The stalkers believe that they are eternally linked to their victims. Researchers believe that this fascination with another person is a sign of low self-esteem.[2] This may be true. People who think well of themselves do not hang on every word and movement of another or believe that their whole destiny resides in him or her.

Most stalkers are thought of as loners who do not associate much with or confide in other people. Loners may also have uncommon interests or hobbies that tend to be outside of the mainstream.

*J*ohn Hinckley, Jr., left, tried to assassinate President Ronald Reagan to impress actress Jodie Foster, whom he had been stalking.

One researcher has compiled a list of several common characteristics among stalkers, including an interest in weapons, death, suicide, religion, and destiny or fate.[3] Many ordinary people also have an interest in such things, but not to the extent that they assume that other people are equally interested or somehow involved in them. The stalker may transfer a fascination or intense interest in something to the victim, and assume that they are alike.

Stalker Profiles

There is no standard profile of a stalker. He or she may range from a cold-blooded killer to a teenager with a crush on a teacher. Several model descriptions have been made, however, and they all have elements of truth. Most stalkers are known to their victims, either as former spouses or dating partners. They have in common many of the following characteristics or personality traits:

> Low self-esteem

> Feelings of dependency

> Tendency to view people as possessions

> Fears of abandonment

> Feelings of severe jealousy

> Irritability

> Alcohol problems (40 percent)[4]

This last trait, a dependence on alcohol (or any other drug), seems to indicate that stalking is another form of antisocial or erratic behavior. Indeed, most of the list can be applied to anyone who commits any crime. What is missing from this list is the matter of obsession. Stalkers are driven to do what they do by an overwhelming need to punish or to be with another person. Jealousy might be the most important of the traits listed, since it includes possessiveness and obsession. The stalker cannot give up his or her imagined or former lover and cannot stand to see him or her involved with someone else. A wish for revenge also enters the picture. Stalking is considered a progressive behavior problem. This obsessive and possessive behavior is most likely to lead to violence over a period of time.

Most stalkers do not possess strong social skills. They are loners who do not interact with other people in a normal way. In other words, they act in strange ways that make other people uncomfortable. One of the strongest pieces of advice that stalking experts give to a victim is to trust his or her instincts.[5] If anyone makes a person feel uncomfortable or frightened, that person should be avoided at all costs.

There may be no standard profile of a stalker, but most professionals would agree on one thing: They all have mental problems. Mental illness can be loosely defined as the inability to keep a mental balance during periods of emotional stress.[6] For example, some people are overwhelmed by relatively trivial events such as family quarrels or failing a test. A personality disorder occurs when a person's individual traits repeatedly bring him or her into conflict with relatives and acquaintances, or in some cases, with outsiders.[7] "Stalkers seem to have both a mental illness and a personality disorder," says psychiatrist Dr. J. Reid Meloy. Those who stalk strangers are more likely to have severe mental

*M*argaret Ray, who suffered from schizophrenia, stalked David Letterman for many years. In this 1997 photograph, Ray appeared in a Florida court on charges that she was stalking former astronaut Story Musgrave. Ray took her own life on October 5, 1998.

disorders than those who stalk former spouses or sexual partners, he adds.[8]

Dr. Kristine K. Kienlen is a psychologist at the Minnesota Security Hospital in St. Peter, Minnesota. She treats criminals and persons who are mentally ill and possibly dangerous. She recently studied the backgrounds and profiles of stalkers and believes that their behavior might stem from what psychologists call an attachment disorder.[9] Attachment disorder is a condition that causes a person to have difficulty in forming loving, lasting relationships. The person is unable to trust other people or to be genuinely affectionate with them. People who suffer from attachment disorder usually fail to develop a conscience.[10] An attachment disorder may stem from a childhood lacking a parent or caring adult.

Cyberstalking

The crime of stalking entered a new phase with the growing popularity and use of the Internet. Stalkers have used newsgroups and chat rooms to harass their victims. "The same traditional crimes are being committed in a new environment where the criminals are allowed anonymity,"[11] says one investigator. One such stalker is Kevin Massey, who harassed Robert Maynard, the founder of Dallas's Internet America, an Internet provider like America Online. Massey sent Maynard messages claiming that Maynard's employees were liars and were attacking him in online messages. He also accused Maynard's wife of being unfaithful, and appeared to threaten violence by sending the message "I have a .45 [pistol]."[12] Maynard sought legal action and a judge granted a restraining order against Massey, who was then known only as "Mackdaddy" and other computer-related names he used in his messages. When Massey was discovered as the source of the messages, he was happy with the publicity. He now calls himself the "Cyberstalker" and makes himself available to talk show interviewers and anyone else who will listen to him.[13]

The complete anonymity of the Internet and e-mail may encourage stalkers who are afraid or unable to actually follow or harass their victims in person. The Internet also allows stalkers access to private information about their victims. With their computers they can spread tales, make threats, cause fear, and generally make life miserable for whomever they have targeted. And they are very hard to catch. Most police officers do not know enough about the Internet or e-mail to do anything about the complaints they receive. Special units are being set up in many police departments to deal with computer crimes, but they are expensive and require extensive special training. The law will probably be slow in catching up with the cyberstalkers, but things are looking up. The restraining order against Kevin Massey, for instance, was delivered by the court over the Internet.

In the meantime, the only way to protect oneself against Internet stalkers is to be very wary of chat rooms, newsgroups, or special interest groups that request a street address, phone number, credit card information, or anything else of a personal nature. Also, treat the Internet in the same way as personal columns in newspapers and magazines, dating services, or "lonely hearts clubs."

There is a positive side to the Internet, however. There are online support groups for anyone who is being stalked, has been stalked, or is in fear of being stalked. Some parents, teachers, or friends—not to mention police—still refuse to take a person's claim of being stalked seriously. Legitimate Internet support groups such as Survivors Of Stalking, Inc., can reassure stalking victims that they are not imagining things. These groups also provide free publications and services that could convince reluctant parents or officials of the seriousness of the problem.

Chapter 3

Anatomy of a Stalker

There are two general types of stalkers. The first and more common type is often called "simple obsessional." The majority stalk former spouses or dating partners. The stalker's motive may be to force the victim back into the relationship or to get revenge by making the victim's life miserable. These stalkers are also possessive and believe that they own the subject of their love. Most researchers consider stalking a behavior problem that worsens over time. In extreme cases, stalkers may stop at nothing to take possession of the person they obsess about.[1] They may kidnap, severely beat, or even murder their victim. It is estimated that 90 percent of women killed by former or estranged husbands or boyfriends were stalked before they were murdered.[2]

Charlotte Garner was stalked for seven years by her ex-husband after their divorce. During that time, Joseph Garner repeatedly broke into Charlotte's home and beat her. He often threatened to kill her, their three children, and himself. Joseph Garner was finally arrested by Indianapolis police in

Three Types of Stalkers

Psychologist Dr. Kristine K. Kienlen has encountered three kinds of attachment-disordered stalkers in her research:

The "Preoccupied" Stalker: Has poor self-image but admires other people unlike her- or himself and seeks their approval to feel good. If approval does not come, he or she stalks to restore confidence.

The "Fearful" Stalker: Also has a poor self-image but does not think well of other people. This stalker longs for the approval of others, but does not think much of it because it comes from people he or she distrusts. The person stalks to boost his or her sinking ego.

The "Dismissing" Stalker: Has a high self-image and does not seek the approval of others, since the person considers them beneath him or her. When the stalker is rejected, he or she stalks out of revenge for being mistreated.

Source: Jane E. Brody, "Researchers Unravel the Motives of Stalkers," *The New York Times*, August 25, 1998, p. F7.

December 1995. However, his arrest was not for stalking his ex-wife but for allegedly murdering his seventy-six-year-old father. Garner had stabbed his father more than two hundred times. In 1997, a jury found Garner guilty but mentally ill. He was sentenced to sixty-two years in prison.[3]

The second type of stalker is the love-obsessed stalker. Many of these stalkers suffer from mental illness. Their behavior is usually chronic, which means that it does not change. They continue stalking no matter what measures are taken against them.

Unlike the simple-obsessional stalkers, there is no prior relationship between the stalker and the victim. However, the stalker believes that he or she is destined to be with the victim. The stalker believes that if he or she pursues the victim long enough and hard enough, the victim will come to love him or her in return.[4] Some of these stalkers are called "erotomanic." They falsely believe that their victims are attracted to them, or even love them.[5] These stalkers develop an extraordinary sensitivity to cues that most people would otherwise dismiss. If their victim smiles at them, they may take it as a sign of love. Included in this group are the celebrity stalkers, who receive a great deal of media attention.

In the 1980s, Ralph Nau began a long obsession with singer Olivia Newton-John. Although he had never met the entertainer, he was convinced that she was in love with him. Nau believed that Newton-John's movies and records contained secret romantic messages meant only for him. He followed her around the world, from Los Angeles to Australia. Nau was eventually arrested in Wisconsin for

*O*livia Newton-John was stalked by a man who believed that she was sending him secret romantic messages in her songs and movies.

murdering his stepbrother with an ax. Although the charges for the murder were later dropped, the state committed Nau to a mental hospital.[6]

Stalking's Three Phases

Both types of stalkers are generally unpredictable in their behavior. However, certain patterns have emerged. There are usually three phases of stalking.[7] The first is when the stalker makes his or her presence known to his victim. This can be anything from an approach on the steps of the town library, as in the case of Barbara Wickens, or a simple phone call or letter. If the victim does not respond to the stalker's advances or turns him or her down, the stalker's obsession may increase and lead to more aggressive or violent action. The stalker may now actively follow the victim and even appear at his or her home or workplace. The stalker may often make his or her presence known by vandalizing the victim's property. The stalker lets the victim know that he or she is out there, watching and waiting.

Next is the explosive or violent phase, when the stalker loses control and makes threats or actually resorts to physical abuse or, in extreme cases, to rape, kidnapping, or murder. This is the worst part of the whole cycle and the only one that law enforcement agencies seem able to deal with. Unfortunately, it is often too late for them to prevent an attack. All the police can do is arrest the stalker after the damage has been done.

The third phase has been called "the hearts and flowers phase." The stalker may become sorry for an action and seek forgiveness from the victim by sending flowers, gifts, or letters of apology. If no violence has already been done, this can occur between the first and second phase. However, it is usually a good sign that the stalker is losing control or is already out of control. Unfortunately, this phase may give the victim a feeling of relief that the nightmare is over, that the stalker has given up. The victim may actually feel sorry for the stalker and even agree to form a friendship or at least adopt a "let bygones be bygones" attitude. This may be the worst thing a victim could do, because it will only encourage the stalker in his or her obsession.

There are probably endless variations on these three phases, but one thing is clear: Stalking is a progressive condition.[8] It does not stop, and it usually gets worse. In some cases, stalkers were warned off successfully, but then transferred their obsession to someone else. Or the victim has moved to another city or state or country, in which case the stalker finds someone new. In some cases, the stalker has followed his victim relentlessly from town to town.

The lesson in all this is for the victim to never let his or her guard down. The law has slowly begun to become aware of the criminal aspects of stalking. However, until a full-scale effort is made to recognize and prevent stalking before it can result in tragedy, the only thing one can do is recognize it and try to avoid it as soon as possible.

Chapter 4

The Victims of Stalkers

When stalking makes news, the reason is usually that the victim is a prominent or well-known person. To the media and to its audience, that seems reason enough to explain the stalker's actions. A person's celebrity or fame can attract all sorts of people—fans, admirers, imitators, and, unfortunately, stalkers. So it seems to many people that celebrities are victims of stalkers simply because of their fame and familiarity. They are easily recognized, their movements are usually known, and they are usually approachable.

Celebrities, however, make up only a small part of the 8.2 million women and 2 million men who have been stalked at some time in their lives.[1] When a stalking incident occurs that does not involve a celebrity, the media and law enforcement agencies usually pay more attention to the stalker than to the victim. Who is the stalker? What caused the stalker's behavior? And how can the stalker's behavior be stopped or changed? He or, sometimes, she is the center of their interest.

Only recently have researchers turned to a

Stalking Behaviors

The National Institute of Justice's stalking survey indicated that stalkers behaved in ways that induced fear, although they did not always make threats against their victims.

- ✓ Stalkers made overt threats to about 45 percent of victims.
- ✓ Stalkers spied on or followed about 75 percent of victims.
- ✓ Stalkers vandalized the property of about 30 percent of victims.
- ✓ Stalkers threatened to kill, or killed, the pets of about 10 percent of victims.

Source: Patricia Tjaden, *The Crime of Stalking: How Big Is the Problem?* (Washington, D.C.: National Institute of Justice, 1997) p. 2.

consideration of the victims of stalkers. They believe that to understand why stalking happens, it would help to know what sort of person is being stalked. They found that victims of stalkers fall into three broad categories.[2]

Victims of a Prior Intimate Relationship

This means that the victim was an ex-spouse or ex-lover. This category of victims is the largest and includes separated or divorced couples, sexual partners who have quarreled or broken up, and dating partners who have ended their relationship.

The victims' ex-partners simply refuse to give them up. They follow their victims, call them on the telephone at all hours, park outside their houses or apartments, send them letters, or break into their residences and leave evidence of their calling.

Victims of a Prior Acquaintance

In this category, the victims are usually women who have somehow offended persons who desire their affection or just their acquaintance or approval. This offense can be as simple as the turning down of a date request or even being unaware of the other person's existence. The stalker comes to bear a grudge against the victim and yearns to "get even" or "teach her a lesson." Not all these grudges are the result of a romantic interest in the victim. Neighbors may become offended because the victim is careless of property rights or damages their lawn or car or some other possession. Fellow workers may become offended because the victim is careless or thoughtless of other people's feelings. In most cases, the victims are unaware of the offense or of the seriousness with which it is taken until they realize that they are being stalked.

Victims of Strangers

This category is hardest to define because the victims can be anybody. He or she may be a cheerleader, a math wizard, the most popular student in school, or just anybody who is noticeable. The stalker's identity is unknown to the victim. The victims do not know they are being stalked until the stalkers reveal themselves. They usually do this through anonymous phone calls and letters or by following their victims. Since the victims do not

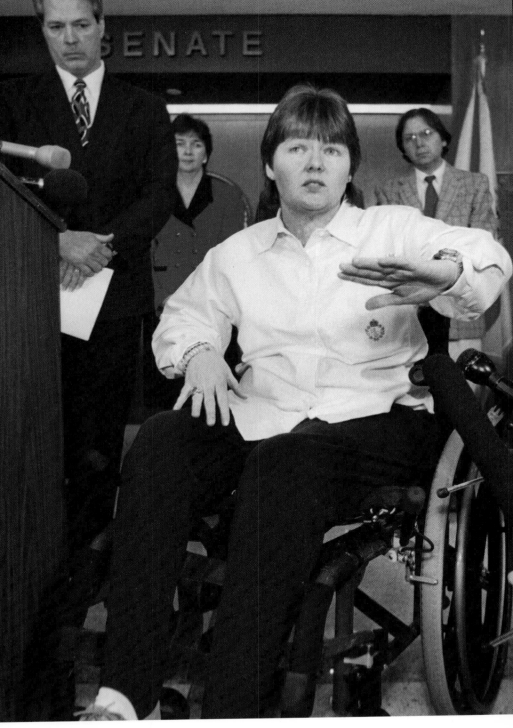

*K*athy Haley was stalked by her estranged husband before he shot and paralyzed her. Here, Haley tries to earn support for a bill that would give unemployment compensation benefits to victims of domestic violence.

know the stalker, they cannot explain what sort of attraction they may have for him or her.

A great percentage of victims of stalkers have described themselves as friendly and outgoing.[3] This in itself may have led them to become victims. A stalker may have misread some signs from the victim and imagined some affection or familiarity on his or her part. On the other hand, someone who acts aloof and suspicious may cause the stalker to become resentful and vengeful. "She won't give me a chance" or "She doesn't trust anybody" may be the stalker's reaction. It appears from the research that there is little in victims' behavior that purposely invites stalking behavior.[4]

Men as Victims

Four times as many women as men are stalked, but this does not mean the problem is any less significant for men than for women.[5] Whereas most women are stalked by men, men are just as likely to be stalked by other men as they are by girls or women. Men find it particularly hard to gain sympathy from friends or action from law enforcement agencies. The feeling seems to be that they can take care of themselves. In one case, the judge told a male victim who complained that he was being stalked by an old girlfriend that he should be "flattered," and issued only a restraining order. Weeks later the stalker killed the young man.[6] Despite cases like this, the general feeling among police and judges is that men are in much less danger from stalkers than women or girls are.

Chapter 5

Stalked and Stalking Teenagers

In 1997, the NIJ issued the National Violence Against Women Survey, which had been conducted by the Center for Policy Research. It claimed that this survey was the first comprehensive and scientific gathering of information about stalking in the United States. "To better understand the broader context of violence in which stalking occurs," the survey states, "the Center for Policy Research collected data from 8,000 women and 8,000 men 18 years of age or older on a broad range of issues related to violence."[1] In other words, the NIJ considers stalking an adult crime.

The fact that the NIJ's survey was limited to those eighteen years old and over is one of the reasons that researchers and experts on stalking believe that the survey's figures are much too low. It has become increasingly obvious that the stalked and the stalkers can be teenage or even younger. In an article for *Maclean's* magazine, Patricia Chisolm calls stalking "the fear that eats at teens. At the very age when girls are becoming women and forging sexual identity," she writes, "the spectre of rape—or worse—is making many fearful of dating, going out at night, even of leaving home to attend university."[2] She quotes Mary Pipher, a clinical psychologist in Lincoln, Nebraska: "It is virtually impossible to overstate how frightened they are."[3]

All children are warned "Never talk to strangers," and "Never get into a car with someone you don't know." These warnings do not seem to have had the desired effect. Children and young teenagers continue to be lured into parks, swimming pools, movies, dances, or rock concerts by older men and women. It is not that the kids are heedless or uncaring but that the stalkers are obsessed, relentless, patient, charming, intelligent, and cruel. These are difficult qualities for a teen or a preteen to combat.

Teenagers often want to be with people their own age, so they tend to avoid adult supervision. This automatically makes them more vulnerable. Unsupervised parties, dances, and other social

Signs of a Stalker

1. Extreme jealousy and possessiveness
2. A need for control
3. Lack of social skills
4. Obsessive behavior
5. Makes a person feel uncomfortable

Source: Robert L. Snow, *Stopping a Stalker* (New York: Plenum Publishing Corporation, 1998), p. 185.

activities offer perfect opportunities for stalkers looking for victims. Popular culture, from television to magazines, puts great emphasis on dating, engaging in sexual relationships, and living together. A seventeen-year-old boy can be just as obsessive, possessive, jealous, and vengeful as an adult. And when his sixteen-year-old girlfriend tells him that she is no longer interested in going out with him, he is more than likely to think that she is playing hard to get, or is merely teasing him.

A teenage stalker can be just as obsessive, possessive, and vengeful as an adult.

The girl's explanation for the reasons for their break-up does not interest the boy. He will not give her up, so he begins following her everywhere she goes. He may pass her notes in school, or write letters, or ring her doorbell late at night to see if she will come out and talk with him. If she tells her parents about him and they warn him off or report him to the police, he may decide that his actions are not worth the risk. The stalker may turn to something or someone else. However, he may become even more determined to continue on his intended course of action. He has then become a full-fledged stalker. His behavior will intensify as he succeeds or fails in his efforts to gain possession of his girlfriend, who has now become his victim. Whether this chain of events leads to violence or a successful change in his behavior will depend largely on the reaction of his victim, her parents, the police, or the courts. It will seldom depend on the stalker, for he is obsessed and will become only more so.

In an actual case, a teenage stalking victim said that as a result of her ex-boyfriend's obsession, she could not have any friends, male or female. "Everything had to be just him and me," she said. "He'd get real upset if he saw me talking to anyone or if I ever said anything about something I had done before I met him."[4] Any night she was not with him he would call her on the telephone over and over again. If she wanted to talk to someone else she would have to use another phone because he was always calling to check if she was talking to someone else. He finally rammed his car into hers when he saw her in it with another boy. The stalker was becoming violent, and the girl's parents had no choice but to call in the police.

The stalking of teens by other teens often goes unreported, either because it is not taken seriously or because the parents or the teenagers themselves do not want to create a scandal or bring unwanted notice to themselves. The stalking of children or teenagers by adults, however, receives much attention because it horrifies everyone.

A typical case is the one of a thirty-one-year-old man who, after he was divorced from his wife, became attracted to a young, athletic teenage girl he knew. He began to attend all of her athletic events, and then wrote to her, asking for a date. She refused him, but he continued to follow her whenever she appeared in school activities. After four years of this activity, he finally began breaking into her parents'

The stalking of a teenager not only causes fear and unhappiness, it robs the victim of his or her youth.

home and stealing personal items from her bedroom and bathroom. He took her photo album and began returning her pictures to her one at a time.[5] Can you imagine how terrifying this was to the girl? She could not play a sport or open her mail without a feeling of dread. The man was eventually put in the care of a criminal psychologist.

Casebooks are filled with stories like this, but they can only hint at the psychological damage that can be done to the victims. Young stalking victims can fear even leaving their own home, let alone engaging in normal teenage activities. Even if they eventually leave home to attend college or live with a relative in a distant city, they are still haunted by the fear that their stalker may be lingering just around the corner. The stalker of a teenager not only causes fear and anxiety, but robs the victim of his or her youth.

Chapter 6

Celebrity Stalkers

Stalking owes most of its public awareness and notoriety to the fact that famous people—notably movie, television, and music stars—have been victims of it. Also, politicians and others who have been featured in any medium are likely candidates for stalking. To the average person, the very thought of following a politician or a rock star from city to city, or camping outside of his or her home, would seem ridiculous. But stalkers are not average people.

With the increasing influence of the popular media—especially television—on the lives of people around the world, celebrities have become more familiar to many people than their own families. This familiarity makes them prime targets for stalkers. In the movie *The Fan* (1981), an actress, played by Lauren Bacall, is stalked by an adoring fan. This was the first movie about stalking. It was followed by many others. *The King of Comedy* (1983), although it was meant to be lighthearted, actually prefigured one of the most common types of stalking—that of television personalities. Most recently, another movie called *The Fan* (1996), had a sports fan stalking a popular baseball player. An actress, a TV personality, and a sports figure, all with one thing in common—celebrity and exposure to the public.

"Being a celebrity carries with it a 100 percent risk of being stalked," says Dr. Park Dietz, a psychiatrist who specializes in criminal cases. "Anyone who's ever been on the cover of a magazine has been stalked more than once."[1] In fact, he says, the question with most celebrities is not whether they are being stalked, but by how many stalkers. "One case we studied had 600 active pursuers at once."[2]

The Death of Rebecca Schaeffer

In 1989, twenty-one-year-old actress Rebecca Schaeffer was murdered by nineteen-year-old Robert John Bardo. Bardo had become obsessed with Rebecca Schaeffer when he was sixteen years old. "She just came into my life at the right time," confessed Bardo.[3] He had watched her over and over in the television series *My Sister Sam*, in which she was having her first real success in a career that seemed destined for stardom. "She was bright, beautiful, spunky—I was impressed with her innocence," continued Bardo. "She was like a goddess for me, an icon. . . . I worshipped her."[4]

Bardo's obsessive behavior was not a secret. Like many other stalkers, he was above average in intelligence, but he had dropped out of high school after a series of incidents that marked his abnormal behavior. He wrote letters to his teachers in which he talked about death, killing, and suicide. He stole money from his mother and boarded a bus to Maine to seek out a young girl named Samantha Smith, who had achieved brief fame by writing a letter to the president of the Soviet Union. Samantha had made the mistake of replying to a letter Bardo had written her. Police found him in Maine and sent him back to his home in Arizona.

A letter Bardo had sent to Rebecca Schaeffer was answered routinely by a service she had hired to answer fan mail. Unfortunately, the service signed all such correspondence, "Love, Rebecca." That did it. Now convinced that Schaeffer loved him, Bardo traveled to Los Angeles, where he attempted to enter the studio where *My Sister Sam* was produced. The studio guards stopped him and sent him away. A

*O*bsessed fan Robert Bardo stalked and killed young actress Rebecca Schaeffer. Bardo was sentenced on November 25, 1991, to life in prison without parole.

month later, Bardo returned to the studio, this time carrying a knife. Luckily, the guards intercepted him and again sent him away. Bardo wrote in a letter to his sister, "I have an obsession with the unobtainable. . . . I have to eliminate what I cannot attain."[5]

When Bardo saw Schaeffer in a movie in which she appeared to be in love with an actor, he became furious. Convinced that she had betrayed their love, he decided to punish her. When he read an article in a magazine about a stalker who had attacked and seriously wounded the actress Theresa Saldana, he was inspired to do likewise. He hired a private detective to obtain Schaeffer's address. Schaeffer was not yet rich or famous enough to live in a high-security building. When Bardo rang her doorbell, she answered it herself. Bardo thrust a letter into her hand. She took it and shut the door on him. Bardo wandered around the neighborhood for a while, and then returned to Schaeffer's apartment building. She again answered the door herself. This time, Bardo shot her at point-blank range in the chest. He had obtained the gun by persuading his older brother to buy it for him before he left for Los Angeles. According to witnesses, Schaeffer screamed and then asked, "Why? Why?"[6]

Antistalking Measures

Why, indeed. The Schaeffer murder and the increasing number of stalking episodes involving celebrities led to the establishment in 1990 of the Threat Management Unit of the Los Angeles Police Department. This was the first time that a law enforcement agency had assigned members to deal with stalking cases. Since its beginning in 1990, the unit has handled more than one thousand cases.[7]

Shortly after, the Threat Assessment Group was founded by Dr. Park Dietz, a California psychiatrist who is an expert on stalking. This organization consults with celebrities, corporations, and government agencies that receive threats. In addition, an increasing number of police departments, researchers, experts, and consultants have gathered a great deal of material relating to celebrity stalking.

One of the findings of these law enforcement and consulting organizations is that celebrity stalkers are not obsessed with a particular celebrity, but rather with the whole idea of celebrity. When a celebrity stalker is somehow thwarted, either by the star's security or by legal action, he or she will often start stalking another celebrity. Michael J. Fox, for example, was followed by a determined young woman named Tina Marie Ledbetter, who referred to herself Fox's "Number One Fan." She wrote to Fox sixty-two hundred times in one year, and most of her messages were threatening. When Fox got married to actress Tracy Pollan, Ledbetter told Fox in a letter that if he did not divorce Pollan, he would die. After Micheal J. Fox sought legal protection,

*M*ichael J. Fox's stalker, Tina Marie Ledbetter, transferred her obsession to another actor after Fox sought legal protection.

Ledbetter switched tactics and began pursuing television actor Scott Bakula. Stalkers like Ledbetter are, says Dr. Dietz, "disturbed individuals in search of an identity. They keep file and press clippings as psychic reward for their activity." When they turn violent, it is because they cannot find fulfillment of their romantic notions, rather than because of their love of the celebrity.[8]

Another striking characteristic of the celebrity stalker is that he or she makes contact with the victim, usually by mail, before actually appearing on the scene. This may be because the celebrity is usually well protected or insulated from the public, and telephone calls are easily screened. The stalker therefore persists in his correspondence, usually dwelling on the "special fate" or "destiny" that the stalker and his victim share. The letters may contain specific dates when "something would happen" to the celebrity. The stalker may mention weapons or other means or objects of intimidation. Unfortunately, there is no telling whether the stalker will ever approach the victim or turn violent when he or she does manage to confront the celebrity. The only thing celebrities can do to combat a determined stalker is to increase their security measures.

For the average person, who is just as likely to be stalked as a celebrity, such security is unaffordable. But one positive outcome of the publicity and the sensationalism surrounding celebrity stalking is that law enforcement agencies have been forced to take notice. Stalking has become recognized as a crime, and that means that society should do as much as it can to prevent it.

Chapter 7

Stalking and the Law

California has taken the lead in antistalking legislation. The senseless murder of Rebecca Schaeffer had shocked the people of that state, especially when it was obvious that the justice system could do nothing to prevent such crimes. The law continued to view stalking as a form of domestic violence, which was considered a "private matter," and was something the police could do nothing about until a crime had been committed. Then, within a year of the Rebecca Schaeffer case, four more women in Orange County, California, were killed by stalkers. It was revealed that all four women had sought help from the police. Three of the women had even taken what little legal action was available to them to thwart their tormentors.

Something had to be done. Judge John Watson of the Orange County Superior Court decided to act. He stated that "the way the law was written did not allow us to protect these women. In some of these cases, the police told the women there was nothing they could do until the man committed a criminal act. By then it was too late."[1] Judge Watson helped to write California's landmark antistalking bill, which passed the California legislature in 1990 and became effective on January 1, 1991.

Federal Laws

Following California's lead and responding to pressure from voters and women's groups, state after state passed antistalking laws. In October 1993, Maine became the last of the fifty states to make stalking a crime. Stalking was now against the law in every state of the union, and it now remained for the United States government to make it a federal offense. Beginning in 1994, Congress began passing a series of laws that eventually became known as the Violence Against Women Act (VAWA).[2]

These federal laws are meant to strengthen state laws and allow federal law enforcement agencies, such as the FBI, to take up the case when any of the above laws are broken. The only problem is that all state laws are not alike. In some states, a stalker has to actually follow a victim before he can be restrained or arrested. This means that the stalker could write letters, make phone calls, or lurk outside a victim's home, school, or place of employment. Another state required that a stalker must first be stopped by the police and be warned off before he can be charged with anything. The flaw here is obvious, because the stalker's second attempt could cause injury or even death to the victim. The states are constantly revising their laws and trying to come up with a code that will prevent stalking as well as punish stalkers and yet not violate anyone's rights.

Although antistalking laws are now in place throughout the nation, they do little good if they are not enforced. Too many police departments still

Violence Against Women Act of 1994

Under this act:

✓ It is a federal crime for anyone to cross state lines to do bodily injury to a spouse or intimate partner.

✓ Those who cross state lines to do bodily injury to a spouse or intimate partner can be sentenced to prison for up to ten years if they use dangerous weapons, twenty years if they cause life-threatening injuries, and for life if they kill their victim.

✓ Stalkers and those under court orders to stay away from their victims can be prosecuted as criminals if they travel from one state to another to harass or injure their victims.

✓ Stalkers and those under court orders are restricted from buying firearms. Anyone who has been convicted of any offense involving domestic violence or stalking can be prosecuted for continuing to own or to acquire a firearm.

Source: U.S. Department of Justice, *Violence Against Women Act of 1994*, 1994, <http://www.usdoj.gov/vawo/vawa/vawa.htm> (September 29, 1999).

think of stalking as a minor crime and treat stalkers as petty offenders. When officers apprehend a stalker, the public prosecutor may treat the case lightly and fail to press charges. If the arresting officers can convince the judge to prosecute, he or she may still treat the case like one involving a private, domestic relationship. Judges, who may not understand the psychology of the stalker or the seriousness of his or her obsession, usually set low bail bonds. This easygoing attitude only encourages stalkers and leaves them free to continue their obsessive behavior.

In a notorious case, Brooklyn judge Lorin Duckman released a stalker and woman-beater who was up before him on a charge of violating a protection order. Benito Oliver had been given a short jail sentence for beating up his girlfriend, Galina Komar. When he was released from jail, he began stalking and harassing his now former girl-friend. Komar had been granted a restraining order against Oliver, but he continued to stalk her.

When brought before Judge Duckman, Oliver argued that he was not stalking Komar, but merely trying to get her to return his dog. When Judge Duckman freed Oliver, the prosecuting attorney complained that Oliver had a potential for violence. Judge Duckman claimed there was nothing to worry about. "He has been in jail long enough for a person who is charged with these crimes. I want to know about the dog."[3]

Three weeks later, Oliver followed Komar to the place where she worked and killed her with a shot in the head from a revolver. Judge Duckman's outrageous decision eventually cost him his judgeship, but the damage had been done. His concern for the welfare of a dog over the safety of a battered and stalked woman is an extreme example of the attitude of many judges. They simply do not take these types of cases seriously enough, says district attorney and former judge Jeanine Pirro, "either because these cases were never violations of the law before or because judges fail to understand domestic violence and the pattern of behavior that precedes the ultimate injury."[4]

Even when stalkers are convicted and sent to prison, prison guards and officials consider them harmless compared with the hard cases they have to deal with every day. Parole boards also take a lenient view of stalkers, who are usually polite and well mannered and even model prisoners. Early release is usually the case with stalkers, sometimes with tragic results. In Florida, a woman who stalked a man who had jilted her and then shot him to death served only one year of a fifteen-year sentence. In Indiana, Alan Matheney, who was convicted of viciously beating his wife, continued to stalk her from prison through letters and phone calls, threatening to kill her. Despite this, prison officials considered him a low-risk case and granted him a forty-eight-hour leave. They made him promise, however, to stay away from his by then ex-wife. When released, Matheney promptly stalked his ex-wife and murdered her.

The most notorious case, however, is the attack on tennis star Monica Seles. A man who was obsessed with Seles's main rival, Steffi Graf, stabbed Seles, hoping to put her out of competition with Graf. A German judge found the stalker guilty and sentenced him to two years in prison, but then suspended the sentence and let the man go free. The world was stunned.[5]

When President Clinton signed the Interstate Stalking Punishment and Prevention Act on September 23, 1996, he said, "Today we say loud and clear, if you stalk and harass, the law will follow you wherever you go."[6] But for the law to be effective, the police must act swiftly and decisively. If the stalker is convicted, his punishment must be equal to his or her crime and it should be strictly applied. Until that happens, stalking will continue to be a major social problem. In the meantime, there are things that the victims of stalkers can do to protect themselves.

Chapter 8

What to Do If You Are Stalked

If a person feels or has proof that he or she is being stalked, one of the best defenses is to know the law. The laws against stalking are so new that many police officers are not familiar with them or even know that they exist. If there is enough proof to file a complaint, a person should take a copy of their state law (available by mail or by fax by calling the National Victim Center at 800-394-2255) to show to the police. The victim should make sure that the police take a report and that he or she gets a copy. The copy of the reports helps the victim in case the stalker continues his activity after being warned off by the police. With the previous report in hand, the victim can prove a pattern of behavior on the part of the stalker. The victim should also make sure that the police let the stalker know that they are aware of his actions.

Tell Others

If you feel that you are too young to do all of this yourself, do not hesitate to inform your parents or some other responsible adult of the situation. If they

*P*resident Clinton signed into law the Interstate Stalking Punishment and Prevention Act on September 23, 1996.

themselves are not aware of the law, they should know where to find the basic information. Whatever you do, do not keep your feelings or your fears to yourself. Some young people assume that they have brought their situation upon themselves. Nothing could be further from the truth. Stalkers are disturbed people who seek to control others through fear and intimidation. They do not need sympathy or understanding. They should be avoided, even by taking legal means if necessary.

Get a Restraining Order

If the stalker is still not convinced that you mean business, you may want to obtain a restraining order. A restraining order, issued by a judge, forbids the stalker to have any contact with you. Unfortunately, a restraining order is just a piece of paper and cannot prevent a stalker from approaching you or doing harm to your property or person. It will, however, upgrade the stalker's offense and make his punishment greater if he breaks the order. And if he or she crosses a state line to continue stalking, he or she has then broken a federal law. In other words, a restraining order will not protect you, but it will certainly make things harder for the stalker if he or she commits another offense. This may be enough to discourage minor stalkers who are well known in the community and have good jobs or a social position they want to maintain. But make no mistake, it will not deter the truly obsessed or those bent on revenge or inflicting harm.

Involve Others

There are not enough police officers to provide full protection for every stalking victim. A great

*C*hristopher Bailey, sentenced on May 16, 1995, to life in prison for kidnapping and beating his wife into a coma, was the first person to be convicted under the Violence Against Women Act of 1994.

deal of your safety and well-being will depend on you. Even though you have notified the police and gained all the legal ammunition you may need, you must still be constantly on your guard. By this time you should have told your friends, parents, coworkers, and anyone else you are close to of your suspicions and fears. If possible, get a photograph of your stalker and show it around to let everyone know the person who is harassing you. Find out all you can about him or her and let that be known to persons close to you. Involving others is important. Stalkers, who are usually loners, will probably not approach their victims if they are in the company of two or more people.

Vary Your Schedule

If you are still in school, be sure that you walk to and from school with at least one friend. Keep your parents or another responsible adult informed of your whereabouts at all times. If you must go places alone, be sure that you do not make a pattern of your activities. Vary your schedule and take different routes to wherever you are going. If a stalker cannot be sure where you will be at a certain time, he will have difficulty following or confronting you.

It is important that you never, ever meet with the stalker. "Even if he says it is only to say a final good-bye or to return the victim's belongings. It is most likely a lie and may escalate the problem," says Dr. Doris M. Hall, a professor of Criminal Justice at California State University.[1]

Use New Devices

If you or your parents can afford it, use modern technology such as cellular phones and beepers to let others know if you are being followed or harassed. You can work out a prearranged code in case you are alone at home or in your car or other places where you might be approached by the stalker. Keep extra money on hand in case you have to hail a cab or jump on a bus to get away. Teenagers can carry all sorts of technological devices in their backpacks, or even simple devices such as whistles or battery-powered alarms that can frighten a stalker away. Remember, most stalkers do not like attention of this sort. They depend on low visibility and stealth.

One of the ways many people use to escape their stalkers is simply to move away or get as much distance as they can between them and their tormentors. Parents, if they can afford to, might send their stalked children to private schools. Other victims might move to another city. Some have gone so far as to change their names and looks. Women who are stalked by former spouses are the ones most likely to use this method of obtaining their freedom. This is one of the worst things about

Protect Yourself

The Privacy Rights Clearinghouse at the University of California at San Diego has put together a list of tips for self-protection against stalkers. Some of the most important are:

✓ Keep your address private.

✓ Do not give out your telephone number. Do not print your telephone number on checks.

✓ Guard your e-mail. Change your e-mail address if you believe you are being cyberstalked.

✓ Keep a diary and record every stalking incident and every contact you have made with the police.

✓ Secure your home with dead-bolt locks and alarm systems.

✓ Secure your car or van, keeping it locked at all times. Never park in a parking lot where you have to surrender your keys.

✓ Know the locations of police and fire departments and go there directly when you believe you are being followed.

Source: Jane E. Brody, "Do's and Don'ts for Thwarting Stalkers," *The New York Times*, August 25, 1998, p. F7.

stalking, because it takes away a person's basic rights. We are all supposed to be able to live normal lives, wherever we want, free of fear. Another unfortunate thing about moving away is that it does not always work. Some stalkers are so obsessed that they will hire private detectives to find out where their victims are. But even if fleeing or moving away works, the stalker may simply turn his or her attention to someone else. Nothing will improve until the stalker is either successfully warned off, or, if he persists, is punished accordingly if found guilty of breaking the new antistalking laws.

Stalking is not a new antisocial behavior, but only in the last decade has it become recognized as a crime. Only recently has it become the subject of scientific investigation.[2]

As more becomes known about what drives stalkers to follow this behavior, the chances for identifying and restraining or punishing them become better. At the same time, modern advances in communications and technology have made it easier for stalkers to locate and harass their victims. Modern conveniences such as credit cards, automatic teller machines, the Internet, e-mail, cellular phones, and camcorders make every one of us more vulnerable. Our names, addresses, and even our images are out there and available to anyone who wants to locate us for any number of reasons—including, unfortunately, stalking. Anti-stalking legislation is slowly catching up to other laws in our criminal justice system. Until stalking is treated with the same seriousness as rape or robbery, the best defenses are an awareness of the danger, knowledge of the law, and constant vigilance.

The following organizations provide help to people who are being stalked:

The National Center for Victims of Crime
2111 Wilson Boulevard, Suite 300
Arlington, VA 22201
(800) 394-2255 or (703) 276-2880
E-mail: webmaster@mail.nvc.org
<http://www.nvc.org>

The National Organization for Victim Assistance (NOVA)
1757 Park Road, N.W.
Washington, DC 20010
(202) 232-6682
E-mail: nova@try-nova.org
<http://www.try-nova.org>

U.S. Department of Justice / Office for Victims of Crimes
810 Seventh Street, N.W.
Washington, DC, 20531
(800) 627-6872
<http://www.ojp.usdoj.gov/ovc>

Chapter 4. The Victims of Stalkers

1. Patricia Tjaden and Nancy Thoennes, *Stalking in America: Finds from the National Violence Against Women Survey* (Washington, D.C.: National Institute of Justice and Centers for Disease Control and Prevention, 1998).

2. Doris M. Hall, "The Victims of Stalking," *The Psychology of Stalking: Clinical and Forensic Perspectives* (New York: Academic Press, 1998), pp. 117–118.

3. Ibid., p. 134.

4. Ibid., pp. 135–136.

5. Tjaden and Thoennes.

6. Hall, p. 119.

Chapter 5. Stalked and Stalking Teenagers

1. Patricia Tjaden, "The Crime of Stalking: How Big Is the Problem?" *National Institute of Justice Research Preview*, November 1997, p. 1.

2. Patricia Chisolm, "The Fear That Eats at Teens," *Maclean's*, June 26, 1995, p. 36.

3. Ibid.

4. Robert L. Snow, *Stopping a Stalker: A Cop's Guide to Making the System Work for You* (New York: Plenum Publishing Corporation, 1998), p. 66.

5. Jane E. Brody, "Researchers Unravel the Motives of Stalkers," *The New York Times*, August 25, 1998, p. F7.

Chapter 6. Celebrity Stalkers

1. Lorraine Ali, "Stalkers: Is the Threat to Rock Stars Growing?" *Rolling Stone*, November 14, 1996, p. 29.

2. Ibid., p. 30.

3. Mike Tharp, "In the Mind of a Stalker," *U.S. News & World Report*, February 17, 1992, p. 30.

4. Ibid.

5. John E. Douglas, *Obsession: The FBI's Legendary Profiler Probes the Psyches of Killers, Rapists, and Stalkers and Their Victims and Tells How to Fight Back* (New York: Scribners, 1998), p. 261.

6. Robert L. Snow, *Stopping a Stalker: A Cop's Guide to Making the System Work for You* (New York: Plenum Publishing Corporation, 1998), p. 74.

7. Ibid., p. 75.

8. Ibid.

Chapter 7. Stalking and the Law

1. Robert L. Snow, *Stopping a Stalker: A Cop's Guide to Making the System Work for You* (New York: Plenum Publishing Corporation, 1998), p. 169.

2. U.S. Department of Justice, Violence Against Women Act of 1994, 1994, <http://www.usdoj.gov/vawo/vawa/vawa.htm> (September 29, 1999).

3. Gary Spencer, "N.Y. Court of Appeals Removes Judge Duckman From the Bench," *New York Law Journal*, July 8, 1998, <http://www.nylj.com/links/duckman.html> (September 28, 1999).

4. Ibid.

5. Snow, p. 176.

6. Ibid., p. 177.

Chapter 8. What to Do If You Are Stalked

1. Jane E. Brody, "Researchers Unravel the Motives of Stalkers," *The New York Times*, August 25, 1998, p. F7.

2. J. Reid Meloy, ed., *The Psychology of Stalking: Clinical and Forensic Perspectives* (New York: Academic Press, 1998), p. xix.

Kamiker, Laura. *Everything You Need to Know About Dealing with Sexual Assault*. New York: Rosen Publishing Group, Inc., 1998.

Landau, Elaine. *Stalking*. New York: Franklin Watts, 1996.

LaValle, John. *Everything You Need to Know When You Are the Male Survivor of Rape or Sexual Assault*. New York: Rosen Publishing Group, 1997.

Markman, M.D., Ronald, and Ron Labrecque. *Obsessed: The Stalking of Theresa Saldana*. New York: William Morrow, 1994.

Snow, Robert L. *Stopping a Stalker: A Cop's Guide to Making the System Work for You*. New York: Plenum Publishing Corporation, 1998.

Williams, Mary E. *Date Rape*. San Diego, Calif.: Greenhaven Press, Inc., 1997

———. *Sexual Violence*. San Diego, Calif.: Greenhaven Press, Inc., 1997.

Wolff, Lisa. *Violence Against Women*. San Diego, Calif.: Lucent Books, 1998.

A

antistalking laws, 10, 12–13, 45–46, 50, 51, 53, 57
attachment disorder, 19–20

B

Bardo, John, 40–42

C

Center for Policy Research, 33
Chapman, Mark David, 11
Chisolm, Patricia, 33
Clinton, Bill, 50
cyberstalkers, 19–20

D

Dietz, Park, 40, 42, 43
Duckman, Lorin, 48–49

F

Foster, Jodie, 11
Fox, Michael, J., 43

G

Garner, Charlotte, 22, 24
Garner, John, 22, 24
Graf, Steffi, 10, 49

H

Hall, Doris M., 55
Hinckley, John Jr., 11

I

Internet, 19–21, 57
Interstate Stalking Punishment and Prevention Act, 50

K

Kienlen, Kristine K., 19
Komar, Galina, 48

L

Ledbetter, Tina Marie, 43
Lennon, John, 11, 14
Letterman, David, 10

M

Madonna, 10
Massey, Kevin, 19–20
Matheney, Alan, 49
Maynard, Robert, 19

Meloy, J. Reid, 17

N

National Institute of Justice (NIJ), 12, 33
National Victim Center, 51
Nau, Ralph, 24, 26
Newton-John, Olivia, 24

O

obsession, 14–15, 16–17, 22, 24, 26, 27, 34, 35, 36, 40, 41, 42–43, 48, 49, 53, 57
Oliver, Benito, 48

P

personality disorder, 17
Pipher, Mary, 34
Pirro, Jeanine, 49
Pollan, Tracy, 43
profile of a stalker, 16–17, 19

R

Reagan, Ronald, 11, 14
restraining order, 19, 20, 32, 46, 48, 53, 57

S

Schaeffer, Rebecca, 10, 40–42, 45
Seles, Monica, 10, 49
Snow, Robert L., 8
Spielberg, Steven, 10
stalking
    defined, 8–10
    phases of, 26–27
Survivors of Stalking, Inc., 21

T

Threat Management Unit, Los Angeles, 42
types of stalkers, 22, 24

V

Violence Against Women Act (VAWA), 13, 46

W

Watson, John, 45–46
Wickens, Barbara, 7–8, 26

Index